This book belongs to

_____

TELLING TIME WITH GOOFY

Disney's

READ and GROW LIBRARY

Published by Advance Publishers
Winter Park, Florida

Written by Joanne Mattern   Edited by Bonnie Brook
Penciled by Edwards Artistic Services   Painted by Edwards Artistic Services
Designed by Design Five
Cover art by Peter Emslie
Cover design by Irene Yap

ISBN: 1-885222-82-3
10 9 8 7 6 5 4 3 2 1

Goofy woke up and turned on the radio beside his bed.

"The time is now eight o'clock," the announcer said.

"Oh, no!" Goofy shouted. He jumped out of bed.
"I'm late! I'm late!"

Clothes flew everywhere as Goofy got dressed. He was in such a hurry, he put his shirt on backward and put his head through the armhole of his vest. Just then, the doorbell rang.

"I'm coming!" Goofy shouted. He ran to the door in his socks, slipping and sliding over the floor. When he opened the door, Mickey Mouse stood outside with his nephews, Morty and Ferdie.

"What's the matter, Goofy?" Mickey asked as he and his nephews came inside. "You look like you're in a big hurry."

"I am," Goofy said. "I was supposed to be somewhere at 6:00 P.M., but I woke up at 8:00. Now I'm late!"

Morty and Ferdie giggled. "Goofy, 6:00 P.M. means 6:00 at night, not 6:00 in the morning," Morty said.

"That's right," Mickey said. "All the hours between midnight and noon are called 'A.M.' All the hours between noon and midnight are called 'P.M.'" Mickey looked at the clock. "It is 8:15 in the morning now, so that means it's 8:15 A.M. Many hours have to pass before it's 6:00 P.M."

Goofy sat down and sighed. "What a relief! I was sure I was late."

"What's happening at 6:00, Goofy?" asked Ferdie.

"Gawrsh, I forgot," Goofy said.

"I know what's happening at 6:00!" Morty exclaimed. "It's the — "

Mickey put his finger to his lips. "Let's see if Goofy can remember by himself," he said to his nephews.

"Okay," Morty said, smiling.

Goofy shook his head. "All I remember is something important is happening at 6:00. What if I forget when 6:00 is? I'm not very good at telling time."

"Would you like me to stay with you today?" Mickey asked. "I'll help you tell time."

"Thanks, Mickey!" Goofy said with a big smile. "That would be great!"

"It's 8:30 now," Mickey said. "That means it's thirty minutes after 8:00. The little hand shows the hour, the big hand shows the minutes.

"Morty and Ferdie have to be at school at 8:45. That's in fifteen minutes," Mickey told him. "Do you want to walk to school with us?"

"Sure," Goofy said.

The walk to school only took a few minutes. Along the way, they passed a store with a clock in the window.

"That's a digital clock," Mickey said. "It doesn't use big and little hands to point to the hours and minutes. Instead, it uses numbers. The first numbers tell you the hour. The second numbers tell you how many minutes past the hour it is."

"8:35," Goofy read. "That means it's thirty-five minutes after eight."

8:35

9

"There are sixty minutes in an hour," Ferdie added. "After eight o'clock comes nine o'clock, then ten, eleven, and twelve."

"It's just like counting," Goofy said. "That's easy!"

Mickey and Goofy waved good-bye to Mickey's nephews at the school gate. Then they started back home.

Now the clock in the store window said 8:55.
"See, Goofy?" Mickey explained. "It's fifty-five minutes past eight. In five more minutes, it'll be nine o'clock."

"Time for breakfast!" Goofy shouted.

When they got back to his house, Goofy fixed a big
breakfast for himself and Mickey. He was so busy looking
at the clock that he cracked the eggs onto the counter
instead of in the frying pan, spilled orange juice all over
the floor, and flipped the pancakes right up to the ceiling!

By the time they finished eating and washing all the dishes, it was 10:00.

"I need to clean the house this morning," Goofy said. "Will you help me, Mickey?"

"Sure," Mickey said. "Let's listen to some music while we work." He walked over to Goofy's music collection and picked out a tape. Marching band music filled the room.

"It sounds like a parade!" Goofy said.

Goofy washed the windows and mopped the floor.

"That was fun!" Goofy said when they had finished. "What time is it now, Mickey?"

"It's 11:00," Mickey said. "What do you want to do?"

"Let's draw a picture," Goofy said.

A little while later, Mickey held up his picture. "It's a parade," he said. "Look, here you are, and here are Morty and Ferdie and me. What do you think?"

"I think that marching band music has made you think about parades," Goofy said, laughing. "I love parades. Maybe I'll draw one, too."

After a while, Mickey looked at the clock. "Look, Goofy," he said. "It's 12:00, also called noon. After noon, the hours are called 'P.M.' instead of 'A.M.'"

"I know what else happens at 12:00," Goofy said. "It's time to eat lunch."

"Let's go downtown and eat at Joe's," Mickey said.

The two friends walked downtown. "Look, Mickey,"
Goofy said. "Those men are decorating the street."

Sure enough, men were tying colorful streamers
around the lampposts and hanging flags.

"What do you think all this is for?" Mickey asked.

"I don't know, but it looks like fun!" Goofy answered.

Inside Joe's Cafe, Mickey and Goofy saw Minnie Mouse sitting at the counter. They sat down beside her.

"Today I'm teaching Goofy how to tell time," Mickey told Minnie. "He knows something important is happening at 6:00, and he doesn't want to miss it."

"That's right," Goofy said, as he bit into his sandwich. "The only problem is, I don't remember what's going to happen at 6:00."

Mickey winked at Minnie and put a finger to his lips. "I'm trying to help him remember," he said to her.

Minnie smiled. "Good luck," she said. "I have to go now. I have a lot to do today. Good-bye!"

After lunch, Mickey and Goofy walked back to Goofy's house. When they got inside, Goofy ran to look at the clock. "1:30," he said. "Thirty minutes after one o'clock. We still have time before 6:00 comes, don't we?"

"That's right," Mickey said. "Let's read a book for a while."

Mickey walked over to the bookcase and looked at all of Goofy's books. Finally he came back holding a book called *The Big Parade*. It was all about a little boy who marched in a parade in the big city.

"What a great story," Goofy said when they had finished. "I'd love to march in a parade someday."

"Now it's 2:15," Mickey said. "Morty and Ferdie get out of school at 2:30. That's in fifteen minutes. It's time to walk over to pick them up."

When Mickey and Goofy got to the school, it was 2:30. Morty and Ferdie were wearing paper hats. "We made these in school today," Morty said.

Mickey whispered in his nephews' ears. The boys nodded their heads. "Okay, Uncle Mickey," Ferdie said.

"What are you talking about?" Goofy asked.

"Oh, nothing," Ferdie said. He and Morty ran up the street toward Goofy's house.

When they reached Goofy's house, it was 3:00. Goofy fixed a snack for all four of them. "My new hat makes me feel like marching in a parade," Ferdie said. "Let's pretend we're in a parade, Morty."

"Good idea," Mickey said, smiling.

Mickey put on Goofy's tape of marching band music. Ferdie grabbed a big spoon and pretended it was a baton. Morty picked up a toy bugle and began to play along with the music. He and Ferdie marched around and around the kitchen. Mickey and Goofy clapped and waved as the boys went by.

Finally, Morty and Ferdie sat down to rest.

"Gawrsh, it must be 6:00 by now," Goofy said.

"No, it's only 4:00," Mickey said. "We have two hours until 6:00 comes."

Goofy looked worried. "I still can't remember what I'm supposed to do at 6:00."

"Let's go downtown," Morty said. "Maybe we'll see something there that will help you remember."

"Okay," Goofy agreed. They all walked downtown.

"Look at that store, Goofy," Ferdie cried. He pointed to the toy store. Its front was covered with flags and colorful streamers. "Does it remind you of anything?"

"No," Goofy said. "But it sure looks pretty!"

Goofy and his friends walked around for a long time.
Finally, Mickey looked at the clock at the center of town.
"It's 5:00," he said. "We have time to go to one more
store." He led the way into the costume shop.

There were lots of interesting
clothes inside.

Mickey picked up a fancy uniform.
A pin on the front read "Grand Marshal
of the Parade." He held the uniform
in front of Goofy.

"Don't you think it's time to
put this on?" he asked Goofy.

"Now I remember!" Goofy shouted. "At 6:00 there's going to be a big parade, and I'm going to be the grand marshal. Why didn't you tell me, Mickey?"

Mickey and his nephews began to laugh. "I tried to tell you all day long," Mickey said.

Goofy and his friends ran all the way home. "Hurry! Hurry!" Goofy shouted when they reached his house. He tried to pull off his shirt so fast, his head got caught in the collar. "Help! I'm stuck!" he yelled. Mickey helped Goofy take his shirt off.

Ferdie and Morty helped Goofy put his pants on the right way. Mickey helped put on Goofy's shoes.

Then Ferdie handed Goofy his tall grand marshal's hat. Goofy pulled it on so fast, it slid down over his eyes. "Help! I can't see!" Goofy yelled, stumbling around the room.

At last Goofy was dressed and ready to go. Ferdie and Morty put on the hats they had made in school, and Mickey pulled on his costume. They hurried downtown.

"I hope we're not too late," Goofy said, as he ran down the street.

Mickey pointed to the town clock. "Look, Goofy, it's 6:00. We made it just in time!"

33

Everyone cheered as Goofy took his place at the front of the parade. Mickey stepped into line next to Minnie Mouse. Morty and Ferdie were right behind them.

Toot-toot-toot! Rat-a-tat-tat! Thumpity-thump! The band played as loud as it could as the parade started. Goofy marched with his head held high. He was very proud to be the grand marshal of this great parade!

The parade marched through all the streets in town.
When they got back to the center of town, it was 7:00.
"That was a lot of fun!" Goofy said.

"The fun isn't over yet," Mickey told him. "Look!" He pointed to the town square. A huge picnic was laid out on tables all along the sidewalk. There were hot dogs and hamburgers, salads and cold drinks.

"What a great day!" Goofy exclaimed after he had finished eating. "Thanks for helping me tell time, Mickey. And thanks for making sure I didn't forget to be in the parade."

"I had fun too, Goofy," Mickey told his friend as they made their way back home. "But next time you have to do something important, maybe you should write a note so you don't forget!"

Goofy waved good-bye to Mickey and his nephews.
Then he went inside his house and got ready for bed.
By the time he put on his pajamas, brushed his teeth,
and washed his face and hands, it was 8:00. Goofy
climbed into bed.

"I sure did a lot of different things between 8:00 A.M. and 8:00 P.M. today," Goofy said as he turned out the light. "I got to be in a parade and have lots of fun with my friends. Best of all, I learned how to tell time!"

As Goofy closed his eyes, he hummed a song he had just made up:

Tick-tock, tick-tock.
Count the numbers on the clock.
Hours and minutes never end.
There's lots of time to spend with friends!

Then Goofy fell asleep with a big smile on his face.